THE ARRANGEMENT 16
THE FERRO FAMILY

BY:

H.M. WARD

www.SexyAwesomeBooks.com

COPYRIGHT

H.M. WARD PRESS
First Edition: August 2014
ISBN: 9781630350369

The Arrangement 16

Chapter 1

As I pace back and forth, I wrap my arms tightly around my middle, covering the tear in my bloody bodysuit. The stupid stage costume is still clinging to me and I shiver, but not because of the temperature. It's Sean.

Since I arrived at the hospital, I've been stuck in the emergency waiting room. It's packed with people; some are press, trying to find out what happened. Hospital security tossed out anyone that shouldn't be here. I'm covered in blood and it's obvious I was with Sean, so they've let me stay, but the hospital staff won't let me see him. Since I'm not his next of kin, they won't tell me crap either. The only thing I know is he was rushed into surgery. I overheard the paramedic say Sean might bleed to death before he even got here. If I'd kept his ring, maybe they would take pity on me. Right now, I look like a crazy clown. My stage makeup is smeared all over my face from wiping away too many tears.

Pacing the floor, I stare into space. My mind is in overload. What I saw cannot be, but I won't allow myself to think about that, not now. There are more pressing matters at hand, more gut wrenching horrors that I may have to face.

Death cannot visit me again, not today. I can't lose Sean. I couldn't bear it.

After all this time, I wasn't certain how I felt about him—about his good and his bad, about the light and the darkness within this man. But now that Sean's time has been cut short, I know exactly how I feel. It's not fair. Some people my age haven't lost a single person and I'm losing everyone I love. My throat tightens at the thought.

Stop it! I scold myself and try to hold it together. *He's not dead. He'll survive, Sean's a fighter, and he will fight. It's what he does best.*

That makes me smile a little. Fighting is so Sean.

There's a burst of noise and then someone shoves through the doors into the ER. Trystan's brown hair hangs in his eyes, wet with rain. The pavement behind him glitters as flashes of fire and the press tries to find out if he is also hurt. They hurl questions at him in a barrage. His bodyguards push people back, and then manage to follow him into the room. Trystan scans the space until his eyes land on me. Without a word, he races over and opens his arms.

I fall against his chest and sob. Trystan's arms wrap around my shoulders as he kisses the top of my head. "He'll be all right."

"You don't know that!" I manage the words between sobs.

Trystan pulls me back and looks me in the eye. "You're right. I don't know shit. I don't know if he'll be all right or not, but I do know that you can survive anything, Avery." When he says my name I feel stronger. The way he looks at me challenges me to collect the strength that is rapidly flowing out of me. I want to crumble in his arms, but I can't do it, not with him looking at me like I'm a pillar of stone.

Sean was accused too many times of being nothing but stone. Is that what life does?

My throat is so tight that I can barely speak. "People break. They can't endure something like this alone."

"You're not alone. You'll never be alone, not as long as I'm around. Do you understand? This isn't the end." I can't look at him anymore. He's so certain and I'm so scared. My gaze lowers to the floor, but he won't let it stay there. Trystan takes my face between his palms and lifts until we're staring at one another. "I know what you're thinking, what you're feeling. She's here and if that happened to her, God—" he presses his eyes closed, blinking hard. "Some people will say they know, but they don't. The thing is, with us—we're so alike—he's your shaft of light in a dark place, he's the cool breeze in the sweltering heat. I know you. I know what you've been through. No matter what happens tonight, I know you can get through this, too. Avery, your story is epic and this isn't the end." He offers a lazy smile.

My hands have found his and in that moment, I believe him. I want things to be all right. I want Sean to live and I want to marry him. "I didn't know how I felt and now that I do, it's too late." A smile tugs at my lips, but I can't hold it in place. I'm so stupid, so very stupid. I let his dark side dictate what happened to us, but it's Sean's sliver of hope, the man behind the mask, that called me to him in the first place. I forsook him when he needed me. Sobs bubble up until I can hardly breathe.

Trystan brushes my hair out of my face, smearing back tears. "It's never too late." He drops his hands and walks over to the counter where a nurse is totally star struck. Trystan's bodyguards are a few feet away, but since he's walked inside, no one has had the audacity to bother him. There are no fans trying to get his attention. They've remained in their seats and a quiet hush overtook the room. The main source of noise comes from the televisions mounted on the walls. News of the shooting traveled fast and by the time we reached the hospital, there were cameras out front, vying to get more information.

A Ferro gets shot at a Trystan Scott concert. It's like a homing device for every news outlet in the country and more of them are arriving every second. Uniformed police officers are guarding the door, making sure that only patients and staff can come and go.

The young nurse is standing there, mouth gaping, her messy blonde hair pulled back into a bun with a pen sticking through the middle. Her purple scrubs make her complexion appear pristine. If I weren't so upset, her expression would be comical.

Trystan takes her hand and turns up his charm. That mop of dark hair glistens as he sweeps it to the side and gives her his full on heart-breaker smile. "You see that woman over there? She's Sean Ferro's fiancée. She's also one of my best friends. She's so worried about Sean that she can't stop crying. Any chance you can help us out and tell her if he's alive?"

The nurse doesn't move. A high-pitched noise comes out of her mouth, and I'm sure she's going to pass out.

Trystan continues, leaning in, saying the

horrible words softly. "The thing is, we're both friends of the family. If he's not going to make it, please give her the chance to say goodbye."

An older heavyset nurse with dark skin and bright red lips is frowning at him. She finally stands, scolding the blonde nurse, causing her to snap back to life and rush off. Meany Nurse shakes her head. "Just because you're a celebrity you think you can go around breaking rules? Well, you can't. Not here. I'm the charge nurse and I say no." It's clear she thinks Trystan leads an easy life—if she only knew.

Trystan smirks and leans forward on the counter, his hair dripping onto her papers. "Listen," he whispers, "I know people here that could make your life so much easier. Plus, I've managed to hide…" his voice drops so low that I can't hear him. The nurse and Trystan glance at me. "She can't know."

The nurse's gaze flicks down Trystan's bare chest. He's wearing an old leather jacket that's soaked. When she raises her eyes, she nods and lifts her hand to press the button to let us through the door. The thing buzzes and when he turns to look at me, his relief is evident.

"Come on."

A familiar face is standing on the opposite side of the doors, her face white as paper. "Trystan?"

Chapter 2

"Mari," I say her name and thank God there wasn't someone else standing there.

"Avery?" She glances at me and then returns her gaze to Trystan. It looks like someone punched her in the stomach.

Trystan turns toward her slowly, his shoulders tense and his eyes widen. Before she can see, he grabs the ring hanging around his neck and yanks it off, breaking the chain, and shoves it in his pocket. Either he grabbed it before coming here or it was in his pocket during the show. The poser smile he wears too often appears as he resumes his normal slacker stance. "Dr. Jennings, how are you this evening?"

She swallows hard and even with everything that's happened tonight, I can put it together. This is the woman that Trystan's in love with, the woman he's mourning. She's also the woman who helped Sean and me when Logan wouldn't —I like her. Did I sleep with her Trystan? I shiver at the thought.

Trystan notices and hands me his jacket. I take it to cover my scantily clad body, but it leaves him bare-chested. Someone gasps, and it sounds a little too orgasmic. That's when a tall, beautiful man walks by and stops in his tracks. His gaze locks on Trystan, and narrows instantly. His voice drips with malice, "You." It's clear that he hates Trystan, too.

Trystan holds up his hands and steps back like he's trying to avoid a fight. "He saved her. Don't do this, Logan."

"Sean almost died because of you!" the man steps toward Trystan. He's obviously a Ferro, despite the lack of introduction. The way he walks, his stance, the way he hates Trystan reminds me of Sean. Under other circumstances, I'd wonder why the Ferro Family hates Trystan—well, all except Bryan and Jon—but I latch onto something else, instead.

"Sean's alive?" I gasp. My hands fly to my mouth and I swallow a sob.

The man in the lab coat and scrubs glares at me. Trystan makes introductions. "Logan Ferro, Avery Stanz. This is Bryan's brother and Sean's cousin. You can see the crazed resemblance, plus he's got that Ferro arrogance they wear so well. Wouldn't you say so, Dr. Jennings?" He glances at her, but Mari's lost her ability to speak. Her eyes lock with his and she stares at him like she's seeing a ghost.

Logan sneers at me, but answers. "Yes, he was fucking lucky." He stares at me for a moment and then adds, "You don't belong here. You're not family and I can't say that Sean is asking for you. Actually, he said the opposite."

"What?" I can't breathe. Sean doesn't want to see me? Pain grips me from the inside and I nearly double over with the shock of it.

"Avery," Mari starts to say softly, trying to comfort me. "He's been through a lot tonight, and many people say things they don't mean. Don't take it to heart."

I wouldn't, but there's no other way to take it. Nodding slowly, I tell them, "The last time he was in the ER, he ripped out his IV and left. If he needs to stay, make sure he's medicated, because if he can walk, he's leaving." I hope Dr. Ferro will tell me if Sean can walk, but he says nothing. The man stares at me like I'm the devil.

Trystan opens his mouth, as if he's ready to tell Logan off, but the doctor grabs him by the wrist and shoves him into an empty room before he can say much. The door swings shut behind them and yelling ensues, but it's too muffled to make out.

Mari looks me over, her eyes dipping to my ripped costume and dried blood. "Are you hurt?"

Lip quivering, I shake my head and tug Trystan's jacket tighter around my waist. "No, I don't think so."

"Come and let me look you over."

I shake my head again, unable to speak. It feels like I've stabbed this woman in the back. I can't take advantage of her kindness. It's wrong.

"I probably shouldn't ask, but I have to

know—Are you with him?" Her lips press together and twitch, like she's trying to smile, but can't.

I can't answer her. The look on her face is horrible, like I drove a lance through her chest. She still loves Trystan, I'm sure of it, but Trystan's here with me. I blink rapidly and wipe at my eyes. "No, I'm not." After a pause, I tell her, "Make sure Sean doesn't leave. He's going to be pissed when he realizes he's in the hospital. He hates this place. Please help him. I should go."

She reaches out for me, but hesitates. Her fingers don't touch my shoulder as she'd planned. Her hand hovers there for a second. "Wait!" I turn back to look at her. "Is he all right? Trystan, I mean."

I nod once, even though he's not. He needs her, but I have no idea what their story is or why they're apart. Mari's gaze lowers and she smiles. "I'm glad he's with you, then. You seem like you'd be good for him."

"I'm not with him." My voice is unsteady and slight. Mari looks at me like she knows better. My gaze drops, before managing to force a smile. "Yeah, I guess everything happens for a reason, right?"

"I suppose so."

I've believed that up until this point, but after Sean taking a bullet for me and running into Trystan's ex, I don't see how the night could get worse. That's when I hear the newscaster. Slowly, I turn and look up at the TV. "Marty Masterson has been identified as the possible shooter at Madison Square Garden at this evening's Trystan Scott concert. The NYPD is conducting a citywide manhunt as we speak."

Chapter 3

Bob rushes toward me. He sees it happening before I feel it. Suddenly, my head is light and I know I'm going to topple over. Trystan's bodyguard catches me in his beefy arms as I sway. I cling to his huge bicep and stammer, "Marty? Did she say Marty did this?" I saw the gun in his hand, at least I thought I did, but I kept thinking I was wrong—I had to be wrong.

With everything that happened, I won't allow the truth to surface in my mind. I can't handle it. Marty is one of my best friends and in the seconds proceeding the shooting, it made sense that all those people were killed because of me.

"Miss Stanz, you need to lie down." Bob tries to steady me, but I swat at him uncertain of what I need or want.

I'm going to fall apart. I can't handle this. Sean won't see me, Mari is Trystan's old flame, and Marty is a homicidal maniac. No! This can't be right.

"I'm fine." I stare at my nails feeling betrayal seep into my heart, even though I can't accept what I'm hearing on the television. Marty is my best friend, how could he do this to me? I start shifting puzzle pieces together. That means he killed Amber and Naked Guy, and all the others. He kept aiming for me, or Sean, and they got in the way.

Mari says soothing words, but I can't hear her. My heart is thumping in my ear, blaring like a train horn burst after burst. "Avery." She says my name loudly, and I glance at her. "Come lie down."

I shake my head and step back. Lifting my hands, I say, "I can't. I have to go. Sean doesn't want me here anyway. I heard Logan. Just keep him safe. Promise me."

Mari looks confused. By the time she figures out that I was here for Sean, not

Trystan, I'm gone. Darting through the front doors, I shove my way past the cameras and blaring lights. I answer no one, and don't stop until I'm in the parking lot and standing in front of Trystan's Hummer. I yank the door open and climb inside.

The driver recognizes me. Looking in the rearview mirror he asks, "Will Mr. Scott be joining us?"

"No, not tonight. Please drive me to Babylon Station, and then come back here."

His brow lifts at the odd request. "The train station?"

"Yeah. I can find my way from there." I don't want to explain where I'm going. It's not my home anymore, but my brain doesn't seem to know that. When my life crashes and burns to ashes, I end up sitting on the curb watching the sun peek over the treetops. It soothes me when nothing else can, when Jones Beach or the cemetery come up short.

The man nods and guides the car into traffic. We take the expressway and then cut over to Deer Park Avenue, following it until we arrive at the train station. When I open the door to slip out, the driver says, "Are you sure you don't want me to take you somewhere else?" It's fairly dark, except for the glow of the platform above and the parking lot lights.

"There isn't anywhere else I'd rather go." I thank him and shut the door. The driver hesitates and then pulls away, leaving me alone in the dark night.

Chapter 4

I wander, not thinking about where I'm going, letting my subconscious mind take over. Before long, I sit down on the curb in front of my parents' house. There's a realty sign on the front lawn with the word SOLD dangling beneath. My stomach twists as I realize it's changing owners again. I wish I could have bought it, but I have no money. I'm a high-dollar call girl, offered a madamship—if that's even what it's called when a hooker interns as a madam—and here I am homeless, helpless.

The void stirs within me. I need something to cling to, something that feels solid. I thought that something was Sean. I loved him. I still do, and now he won't see me. Why would he say that?

Maybe Logan made it up. Maybe he didn't want me near his cousin for some reason, but no logical explanation comes to mind. It sounds like something Sean would say—especially if he doesn't trust himself around me. If I'd taken the shot, I would have asked for him as soon as possible. But that isn't what happened. He pushed me out of the way and the bullet went into him, not me.

Sean was acting smitten before the concert. I knew he was worried that someone would try to hurt me. In so many ways he's been right about everything. I was wrong and naïve. I made promises and then broke them. I said I'd be there for him and I wasn't. Guilt twists inside of me until I'm ready to puke on the lawn. I was the worst kind of friend to him. I didn't keep my word. I promised him that I wanted all of him, the dark, the light, and the monster within. He finally trusted me and gave himself to me, and I couldn't handle it. He was right to hide from me, to push me away. He knew that his demons were bigger than

I'd known.

But now, nearly losing him, I can't bear to think of my life without him. The fact that he's so broken, so miserable that he needs to exert control over a woman to get off frightens me. What happens when that's not enough anymore? That was the reason I backed off, the reason I left him. It felt like I was feeding his darkness instead of saving him from it. I wanted to be the one who brought him through the darkness and back into the light.

I wanted to save him. I still do.

Easy, Avery. He's still breathing. That's enough for tonight—he's alive. Be thankful for what you have. Stay in the moment.

Stay in the moment. I've said that to myself so many times. When life is ready to crush me, when the massive hammer is hanging over my head, I tell myself to live breath by breath. It works, but it's a painful way to live. Sometimes it seems like a happy ending isn't something I'll get. My cards weren't dealt that way, but I won't be given more than I can handle. I can handle this. I can get through this.

I stare blankly for hours, watching the

sunrise over the houses until streaks of pink and gold mingle together and chase away the inky night. When the first ray of light hits my face, I want to cry. Trystan's words come back and I realize how much I've lost tonight.

Pushing up, I decide to go peek in a window. The grass under my feet crunches as I peer into my old home. It's empty. The house sits silently reminding me of better times. This place was my anchor in the storm, and now I have none. As I walk around to the back, an idea forms. I have nowhere to live. I can't go back to the dorm. There's nowhere to sleep and I'm not safe going to any of my usual spots. No one will look for me here, not inside the house.

Before I have time to think about it, my fist smashes through a pane of glass in the kitchen door. I reach in and unlock it, slipping inside before anyone notices me.

I refuse to drift anymore. I refuse to accept this is my life and I have nothing to show for it.

Padding inside, I watch as the morning sun pierces through the blinds, displaying shafts of light on the carpet. The house looks the same as it did when my parents were here. The last owners didn't even change the wallpaper. I wander into the empty living room and sit down. It's not long before I lie on my back and stare at the ceiling.

Closing my eyes, I call out to her, even though I know she can't hear me, "Mom, I need you."

The stillness of the house cocoons me until I fall asleep.

Chapter 5

No one knows where I am and I keep it that way. Trystan still has my cell phone, so no one can track me. The closest they'll get is the train station and I could have gone anywhere from there. It's nightfall by the time I wake up. My face is patterned on one side from the carpet pile. I rub it out and stretch, looking at the clock on the microwave. The dried blood on my clothing cracks and makes my skin itch and I'm so thirsty I could drink a cow. I'd give anything for a glass of cold milk right now. My throat is so dry it feels like I swallowed a flamethrower.

Blinking slowly, it dawns on me—they

left the power on. Maybe the water is on too. Pushing up, I pad down the hallway to my old bathroom and turn the faucet. I expect it to do nothing, but cold, clear water comes pouring out. Yes! After leaning forward, I gulp greedily until my cracked lips no longer sting and my parched throat feels better.

I straighten and look into the mirror in the darkness. A golden streetlight casts a halo on top of my frizzy brown head, and in that moment I look so old. Gazing into the glass, I stare watching my reflection—seeing my mother's face appear, happy and content. Her voice chimes in the back of my mind like a faded memory, half forgotten. I can't quite hear it anymore; I can't remember the way she spoke or that thick Long Island accent. It's vanishing. I'm losing her. The vision fades back into my haggard appearance and I turn away.

I want to see Sean, but I can't go anywhere looking like this. I need money. I refuse to call Black, even though I know she'll give it to me. I want to avoid that day as long as possible. As it is, I'm sure Gabe is out looking for her investment. I bet she kills Marty if the cops don't find him—maybe they already have. My stomach aches as my heart twists. I can't stand this, what Marty did.

After wandering into the kitchen, I sit down on the only chair left in the house. The metal seat is cold and hard, but I don't care. I lean back and stretch, arching my spine and staring at the cupboards. Mom had climbed up onto a stepstool to clean the upper cabinets so many times. She'd tell me it was a breeding ground for dirt. I stare at that spot, gazing at the wooden doors and the soffits above. They've not lived here for a while, but there's no dust up there. It makes me lean forward and look closer. Maybe the old owners cleaned it, but that's not why I'm staring. The upper cabinets are made of wood paneling, a remnant from an old kitchen. The last cupboard hangs at the end of a run of cabinets, jutting out slightly from the rest. It's the style from the time the house was built. I keep staring, not understanding what I'm seeing that bothers me. Something's not right.

The need to touch the panel overcomes me. I slide my chair over to the spot, feeling my mother calling my name as I do so. My skin prickles as the pads of my fingers touch the spot she touched so many times before. I slide my fingertips across the wood, feeling one bump after another. When my hand is at the end of the cabinet I slide it over the molding on the corner. I do it again, then once more. I laugh at myself for being silly. It's like I want to hug this thing. The compulsion to run my palm over the wood strikes me again, so I humor myself and do it one last time. I'm ready to step off the chair, but the panel under my hand shifts slightly.

"Mom, what did you do?" As I say the words, I press my palm on the wood and shift it, making it slide out on one end. It barely moves, but it's enough that I don't need more prodding. Grabbing the trim on the piece of paneling now sticking off the side of the cabinet, I pull hard. The piece moves and opens, revealing a hiding place in the top of the cabinet. I stare, awestruck.

Behind the panel, under layers of dust, are old wine bottles, papers, and a coffee can. I shift through things instantly recognizing my mother's handwriting.

Stuffed in a mason jar, I find a letter sealed in an envelope that was never mailed. I take the note and break the seal, instantly feeling my mother's soft touch on my shoulder.

It's her handwriting. My eyes scan the words:

My dearest,

I don't know if you'll ever find this, but if so it means it's too late for me. I'm so sorry, my love. Take what's here and don't let them find her. I'm so sorry, my love. Please forgive me.

At first I'm shocked to see her handwriting, but my surprise won't lift. Her words seem panicked and her normally elegant handwriting seems messy and hastily written. The letter was meant for someone else, because I don't know what she means. I assumed it was written to Daddy, making the 'her' in the note me.

I turn the paper over, hoping for more on the back, but there's nothing. Quickly, I grab the rest of the jars and cans from the space and shove it shut. Sitting on the living room floor, I empty each can, one by one. There are no more letters to explain, only jars full of money and a set of fake IDs, one with my mother's picture. She looks like me. This must have been taken years before they died, maybe even before I was born. I blink at it, not knowing what to think.

"Mom, what is this?" I shuffle through more papers, and when I open the last envelope I gasp. It's stuffed with one hundred dollar bills. I pull a few out and look at them. They're the old style, but they're real. There must be a few thousand dollars here, easy.

Why didn't she tell me about this? Did she ever try? I think about catching her on the step stool, and she always had a rag in her hand, balanced over that spot, but the contents look as if they've sat untouched for ages.

I don't know what to think. My first reaction is to talk to Sean—he'd know what to do—what this stuff means. I feel overwhelmed. My mother hid this, and from the looks of it, Daddy didn't know. This letter is addressed to him.

I have to spend some of the money. I can't walk around like this covered in a ripped costume stained with blood. I still have Trystan's jacket, but it won't distract people from blood, even in Babylon. I need to blend. Stuffing one of the bills into my pocket, I decide to walk down the street to the little line of shops. I have to buy some clothes and I need to try to see Sean. I need to tell him I've been an ass, but I'm done now. The manhunt for Marty probably ended already. For once, we're safe.

Chapter 6

I know how to be frugal when needed, mom taught me well. A couple of hours later, I'm walking purposefully through the hospital lobby and wondering how far I'll get before someone interferes. There's not a Ferro in sight and Trystan is gone.

I walk into the elevator like I know what I'm doing. Sean must have been admitted last night. I just hope he's still here. I get off at the fourth floor and attempt to walk past the desk when a nurse stops me.

"Excuse me, dear, do you have permission to be here?" The nurse is middle aged with bags under her eyes from a lifetime of working the nightshift.

I walk over to her, ready to cry. The lump in my throat tightens. "I think so. Sean Ferro is on this floor, right?" When she only stares at me with those dark brown eyes, I stammer on, making it up as I go. "Peter called and told me what happened. He said I could come down now. Do I have the right time? Unless, oh God, has something gone wrong?" I start shaking and cover my mouth to muffle a sob.

The nurse comes around the counter. She drapes an arm over my shoulder. "No, honey, I didn't mean to frighten you. He's stable, but he's not on this floor anymore. They moved him to the east wing on five. Would you like me to take you to him? His mother may still be there. She was here earlier."

"Constance was here?" The nurse nods and starts walking me toward the elevator. "Martha, I'll be right back," she calls to another nurse.

When the elevator doors slip shut behind us she says, "It's terrible that no one knew the truth all these years. What that man must have lived through." She shakes her head. "It's clear that you're a friend of the family, because no one calls Pete Ferro, Peter."

"I am. Actually, Sean and I were engaged." I tell her the truth because it's pressing on me so hard that I might burst. "I broke it off with him and then this happened."

The nurse's jaw drops. For a second, she does nothing. Then, suddenly, I'm in a bear hug and smashed against her soft body. "Oh, honey! The guilt you must feel. I can't even imagine it." She prattles on about how it's not my fault and that there's a chance for every couple, something about stars, and I zone out because it's all a lie. Everything she assumes is wrong.

I'm silent, wiping tears that roll down my cheeks until we stop in front of his door. The name plaque says *S Ferr*. She smirks at me. "We took off the last letter so people would leave him alone." When I don't reach for the handle, she prompts me. "Go on honey."

I lift my hand, but it trembles. My fingers rest on the lever, but don't push down. I can't. "What if he doesn't want to see me?"

"*What if,* is a horrible question. Besides, the only way to find out the real answer is to walk into that room. If you want, I'll wait right here, but I don't think he'll protest—not with the amount of medicine he's had. That bullet skimmed his rib and dislodged a chunk of bone. They spent the better part of the morning in surgery removing the shard so it didn't puncture his lung. He's a lucky man—in regard to that, anyway. Go on in and I'll wait here in case he throws you out."

"Really?" She shouldn't be talking to me. I'm not family and I doubt my name is on his papers. For some reason, this woman is being kind to me—me, Avery Nobody, in my jeans and T-shirt, with Trystan's leather jacket over my arm. I don't look like a Ferro. I don't look like anyone who could know him, but she's kind to me regardless.

"Of course, honey. People act real odd after being through something like that, so give him time. A near miss changes people."

I offer a half smile. "Nothing changes Sean."

"That's where you're wrong. That bullet changes everything. You'll see. Go on, I'll wait." I don't know what she means, but I need to talk to him. I need to tell him that I'm sorry, that I should have stood by him.

I crack the door and peer through. There's a dim light glowing, casting shadows on his face. Sean's eyes flutter open and lock on mine. He watches me, saying nothing. My heart pounds harder as I open the door all the way and step inside. "May I come in?"

Sean's gaze flicks to the nurse in the hallway and then back to me. He nods once and lifts a hand, indicating that I should come in and sit across from his bed.

"See, I told you. Whatever quarrel you had is over. Go make up with your man and put that ring back on your finger. Some people never get a second chance. You two are lucky." She closes the door and as soon as it clicks shut, I want to race over to Sean and wrap my arms around him. I was so scared he was gone. The shot still rings in my ears and the whole horrific thing replays behind my eyes over and over again.

Sean is in a hospital robe with an IV in his arm. His dark hair is messy, but those blue eyes are alert and cautious. "Sit." His voice is scratchy, like he needs water.

I take the seat opposite him. The words and fears I'd been holding in come rushing out. "I'm so glad you're all right. When I heard the shot, I thought he hit me, but then you didn't move. I thought he killed you. Sean, things are so complicated, but I know I want you in my life. If you've given up on us, I'll walk out that door and never bother you again, but if for some reason you haven't, if you still love me," pressing my lips together, I get out of my chair and go and kneel next to his bed, "I want to be with you."

We're both quiet for a moment. Despite his stern gaze, I manage to say the rest, "Do you love me? After everything I put us through, and all the promises I broke, I can only beg. I deserted you when you finally trusted me. Sean, I was so scared, but last night frightened me more. I want you on any level you'll have me. I can't live without you, don't you see? You're my other half." Tears are streaming down my face as I speak and my voice becomes softer and softer, but Sean doesn't answer. His dark piercing gaze remains fixated on mine, harsh and unrelenting.

Continuing, I say, "This was my fault and you were trying. I just didn't know what to do—that day in the box, the way you seemed gone. It scared me. I won't lie to you—it was the scariest thing that's ever happened to me. The only thing that frightened me more was seeing you fall last night. I thought you were gone forever. A life without you is impossible. Please tell me that I haven't lost you. Sean, please say something. Either way, put me out of my misery." I squeeze his hand and begin to withdraw mine when he clasps it, holding on tightly.

"It's my fault. He's gone, Avery. I fucked up." Sean tilts his head back into the pillows and looks up at the ceiling. "I didn't think I was capable of fucking things up like this, but it's beyond that. I'm so far gone they should have left me to bleed out on the stage floor. I deserve it. There's nothing that will make up for this."

"What are you talking about? Sean…" I get up and sit on the edge of the bed, thinking he's not as coherent as I thought he was. I examine his face for signs of a head injury, but don't see one. My fingers take hold of his sheet. I pull it down slowly, waiting for him to stop me, but he doesn't.

Sean tries to take a deep breath and winces. That's when he looks at me and I freeze. "Go ahead and look. That's what you want, right? To see if I'm disgusting on the outside now, too."

"Sean!" I can't believe he said that.

He lifts his robe revealing himself along with a bandaged torso. "I survived and he died—it's so wrong." He drops the robe and for a moment I'm afraid. Sean doesn't sound right. He's lucid, but his voice is off. "The fucking bullet misses me, but it didn't miss him. I had a plan, but that asshole didn't give me the chance and the gun. He fucking had the gun." Sean's big blue eyes meet mine. "Tell me you didn't give it to him. Please, tell me that it wasn't you."

Bryan, we're talking about Bryan. I don't understand anything he just said except for the gun. I took it from the cabin. I was afraid they'd find the pilot I killed and blame Sean, so I kept it. I lied to his face over and over again. That gun shot Amanda. That gun was tied to so many bad things, but when Bryan asked for it he told me he had a plan. He also said he wouldn't tell Sean he had it.

Swallowing hard, I say, "Bryan told you?" Oh shit. I stiffen and try to back away, but Sean grabs my wrist.

"I knew Bryan asked for it. Pete asked for it too, but things were better my way. I knew what I was doing, Avery. I trusted you and you gave the gun to him? Fuck. I knew how to live with the scorn and the public ready to tear me apart, but not this. I can't endure this. Avery, they think Bryan did it— they think he killed Amanda. Mother came by a few moments ago and told me everything; so don't pretend that I can't handle it. Don't handle me with kid gloves and come in here pretending to want to patch things up when you're really here to see if it's true."

"If what's true? Sean, I don't know what you're talking about." The machine behind him starts to beep. His heart is racing too fast. I speak quickly, in a soothing voice, realizing that something has him upset, but without access to the rest of the world for a day, I don't know what happened. "Shhhh, it's okay. I'm sorry. It'll be okay."

The beeping stops and he stares at me. "Bryan didn't do it. I can't let him take the blame for it, but they don't listen and Mother let them think it. Hallie. God, the look on her face… It wasn't supposed to go that way. It was my fault, my mistake, and he took the hit. Now he's gone."

It finally sinks in. I blink once, becoming acutely aware of everything. "Are you saying Bryan's dead?"

Sean looks up into my face with sorrow and remorse. "It was my fault. The other night when I left you with Trystan, there was a reason. It didn't play out right. I was trying to help him and I fucked it up, Avery. Everything I touch dies. Everyone around me is poisoned. I can't stand it. It's my fault he's gone too soon. It's my fault he had my gun and everyone thinks he killed Amanda.

"I could live with it, you know. I had a grasp on my identity even though no one else knew. It was fine—they didn't have to know me. I shut them all out, every single one, even you. You were right to walk away. It was your only chance. I can't take you back. I won't. I love you too much. I can't do this again, Avery—I can't." His voice breaks on the last two words and he covers his face with his arm, hiding the tears on his cheek.

Taking his wrist, I lift his arm slightly and peer at him. Those blue eyes catch mine, and I see so much sorrow that I can barely hold his gaze. "I love you, too, and I'm not leaving. Not now, not ever."

His arm slips to his side and his voice picks up a pleading tone. "You have to. I won't marry you, not today, not tomorrow. I can't fathom the life I'm about to have, and to pull you down with me is cruel. It's unfair to you, Avery, and I won't do it. I want you to have the life you dreamed of with the picket fence and the baby playing in the yard. I can see you there. I'll help you get there, but you'll have to go without me. I can't cause you more pain, I couldn't live with myself."

Despite the words, the way he says that I need to stay away, I'm drawn to him. His candor is rare and in these moments I feel more connected to him than ever before. Leaning in closer and closer, my heart pounds harder and harder, until we're lip to lip. Sean stops and I stare into his eyes, certain that I see his soul. He's afraid, so full of fear that he can't speak.

Brushing my fingers along his cheek, I wipe away a tear. "Did you say you love me?"

Sean tries to look away, but I don't let him. Taking his chin in my hand, I pull it back toward me. "Avery, don't."

"I know you're at your breaking point. I see it, my love. Trust me, just a little bit, just for tonight. Say anything, dream anything, and pretend that you have me."

Sean looks hopeful. "You'll stay the night?"

I nod. "If you'll let me."

"What about Scott?"

Smiling at his jealousy, I say, "I love you. Trystan's just my friend. He's not you." Our eyes lock and something in the moment shifts. I see the walls fall and the relief flood from his heart. Guilt flares inside of me. The thing with Trystan isn't clear, I can't tell him that it's possible we slept together and now isn't the time. Sean needs someone. It sounds like his awful mother came in, told him he was responsible for his cousin's death and left.

"Scott said I'd lose you if I wasn't careful, and then he took you away from me. I thought I'd lost you."

"You didn't." I smile down at him.

"I can't keep you." He lifts his hand and gently strokes my cheek. He's hardly ever touched me that way and it sends a shiver through my body. Need flares and I want to be close to him and lay on his chest, but that's not possible. He's bandaged and it would hurt him to press on him there.

"You can, for tonight. I'm yours. I'm your friend, your confidant, maybe even your purchase, if you'd like." I kid about the last part, but he still looks leery. "Sean, accept my help for once. You don't have to fight off your past on your own, and God knows I don't want to be alone either. Let me stay." I kick off my cheap flip-flops and slip into bed with him. I lie on my side and pull the blanket over my jeans, and then prop my head up with my arm until we're eye to eye. "Tell me to stay, Mr. Jones."

The corners of his lips twitch, as if he wants to smile. "I can't. I want to, but I can't."

The IV makes a noise and one of the little bags begins to empty. Sean's eyelids flutter and I know it's pumping him full of something that's going to knock him out. Stroking the side of his face, I whisper it again, commanding him, "Tell me to stay, Sean Ferro. You need me here. Say it."

"No." His dark lashes close and then open, his sapphire eyes locking on mine.

"You need me."

His voice is barely there. "I do."

"Then, tell me to stay."

"I won't."

"You will."

Sean smirks at me and his shoulders relax. The meds hit him hard and it seems like he can breathe easier again. "I've always loved you. You know that, but we have too many demons."

"I have a box we can shove them in." Sean laughs once and then winces. It's so good to see him smile, but I probably shouldn't be making him laugh right now. "I'm so sorry. Are you all right?"

"Yeah, but I can't do that, fuck that hurt."

Something strange occurs to me and I

know what it is. What I just did to him, it's like the power he feels holding a woman within her fear—it's a control thing—but it's more than that. It's erotic. I feel horrible for even thinking it, but I want to make him laugh again. I want to make him writhe with pleasure or pain. Maybe both. I watch him closely and drag a finger over his chest lightly. "Is this what it's like? Feeling what you feel? Doing what you do? I could make you say anything right now, do anything."

He watches me, and I know he's trying to be careful, but the medicine impairs his judgment. He speaks freely. "It's raw power, controlling someone like that."

I hesitate, not certain that I want to cross this line. "It is. Now, tell them that I can stay."

"I can't. I want you to, but I love you too much. You need to go. Stay away from us, all of us. Leave Long Island, Avery. Start over. Please, I'm begging you." And he is, for the first time in a long time, Sean Ferro is begging me to do something, but there's no way I'm leaving him like this. Not now, not ever.

Leaning down, I press my lips to his ear,

kissing him softly. "Tell them that I can stay. It's a command, Sean. Say it. Now." I press the call button on the bed and an intercom comes on. Static buzzes.

Sean watches me closely, his eyes silently begging me not to cross the line, but I already have. In my mind, I can see myself doing it. My fingers are already on the bandaged rib. I watch his eyes as I begin to slowly press, causing pain to shoot through him. He stiffens and grits his jaw, but his gaze remains locked on mine.

A female voice asks, "Yes?"

I respond, "Sean wants me to stay for the night. Is that all right?"

"If that's what Mr. Ferro would like, yes, he can have one guest remain with him. Would you like me to let the staff know that she's staying with you?"

Sean doesn't speak, so I press harder. He grimaces, trying not to give in. I whisper in his ear, making sure my lips touch the sensitive spots, feeling horrible and wonderful at the same time. "Tell her, yes. Say it." I jab hard, once.

Sean's voice comes out loud and clear, almost an eager yell. "Yes!" I remove my hand from his bandages and watch him, feeling cruel and something else—something that scares me—but it tempts me, too. The nurse says she'll bring blankets in a little bit and the intercom goes silent.

Sean is watching me closely, his eyes full of pain and lust. "You shouldn't have done that."

"You would have."

He doesn't deny it. Instead his gaze moves over me slowly, taking me in. "Pain is power and it excites some people."

"Some people, meaning you?"

He nods. "And possibly you. Check and see."

I smile awkwardly. "What do you mean?"

"Are you wet, Avery? Did that little display of control turn you on?" I gape at him, not wanting to answer, but even drugged he recognizes my delay. "Show me. Put your fingers in your panties and then touch them to my mouth. Let me see for myself."

"No."

"We passed that part. Do it." He's stern, but there's no way he can make me, not like this.

I know what it did, but I don't want to share this information. Either way, it's too late. When I fail to move, Sean slips his hand under the hem of my shirt. His sapphire eyes lock on mine as his palm slips over my stomach, then past my waist and lower. My mouth opens and I gasp as he touches me, every bit as sensitive as if I'd been lusting after him for hours. His fingers move and he takes his hand out, bringing his fingers to his lips and licking them one by one.

I laugh. "You're exaggerating, Mr. Jones."

"You have no idea what turns you on, Miss Smith. I think you might be a power junkie, because you are way too wet for that whole little display to not have had any effect on you." He smirks slightly.

"What was that? You think this is funny?" I lean in closer to his face, careful not to lean on him. God, he's beautiful. His scent fills my head and I love moments like this, when he says whatever he's thinking and doesn't hold back. I don't deserve this chance. Last time he put his confidence in me, I pushed him away. I feel bad for a second, like I'm taking advantage of him. He could be pissed about this come morning, but I can't pull away from him. I'm greedy and I'll take what I can get. Life is too short not to.

"No," his voice is light and he smiles at me. "I'm just glad our relationship being in shambles isn't all my fault. Part of it is, I'm certain, but not all of it. You can't be that wet, that turned on by a two second display of pain if it's not hardwired into you."

"That's not true. I was just messing around."

"No, you weren't. And that's what did it, right? It was intentional and there's something wrong with it, right? Baby, I know all about it. You can tell me. You don't have to be afraid of it." His hand strokes my cheek as he pulls me close and kisses me lightly.

His words scare me, but something flutters in my stomach and it's freeing. "It was cruel." Shame flushes my face and I go to push off the bed, but he grabs me.

"I said you could stay, so stay. Use me, if that's what you want. Make me scream out in pain. They'll just give me more meds, and then you can do it again." His eyes sparkle with delight, like he wants me to do it.

But I shy away. "I'm never doing anything like that again. I've hurt you enough to last a lifetime." I pull away, but the words he seeded in my mind make my stomach twist and parts of me tingle even though they shouldn't.

"If we stay together, it'll happen again— to you, to me. You can't hide that forever, Avery. It'll tear you apart inside." Sean's eyes flutter and I know he's not able to stay awake. "I've made mistakes that I can't fix and it kills me. Every time I look at you, I see me a few years before Amanda died and took the baby with her. It was my fault, that's why I let them blame me. I died that day and you've been living with that man's ghost."

"There are days that I can't look in the mirror. I've caused so many people such horrible heartache. They never forgave me, and they shouldn't. I can't forgive me either. I should have gone home that day. I should have noticed, but I didn't. That's what happens to me—everything I touch turns to ash. I've tried so hard not to turn into my father that I never saw I was becoming my mother. She's dead inside. When she came to visit earlier, her idea of a greeting was to kick the bed and ask me if I was still alive. She sounded disappointed when I replied."

Sean blinks slowly at me. "The day that you jumped on the back of my bike, my world was tipped on its side. I've never seen anyone fight for life the way you do. I wish I could be the guy who takes you in his arms and lets you rest. I wish I could ease your pain and make your struggles lessen, but life is pain and by now I know better. I can't go back to who I was, what I was. If I was a little lighter and you were a little darker, maybe we could meet in the middle and have a real chance, but you're the sun and I'm the moon. We chase each other in the sky, but never meet for long. It's not meant to be, no matter how much I love you. I have to let you go. I'm sorry."

His words break the dam that I've been hiding behind and tears flow freely from my eyes. He doesn't notice and keeps talking, jabbing each word deeper into the open wounds. He understands me more than I knew, and he feels so much more than I thought. Sean isn't made of ice like Constance. They're not the same, no matter what he thinks.

"I'm sorry, too—for everything." Sitting next to him on the bed, I stroke his dark hair as he falls asleep. I doubt he'll remember any of this in the morning, but I'll have this memory forever. It's the confession of a man broken to pieces with demons tearing at his soul night and day. There's no peace, no release from the pain that haunts him. He's pushing me away because he doesn't want me to become him.

The thing is, it's too late, because I already am.

Chapter 7

Sean stirs in the early morning, coherent and swearing. He stops, suddenly still. "Avery?"

I'm groggy from lying awake all night, pouring my soul out to him. He'd smile and drift off, happy I was there, but I doubt he recalls a word or any of the gentle kisses we shared. "Good morning, Sean." Pushing up on my elbow, I sit up on the side of the bed. "That four o'clock nurse was mean."

He's on autopilot and his voice sounds cautious. "You're just saying that because she tried to throw you out."

I go from sleepily rubbing my eyes to sitting straight up and gaping at him. How does he remember that? The entire night should be a blur. I try to hide my fear and cover it with a stretch. Sean doesn't notice, or at least I don't think he does. I laugh it off. "Lucky guess. Everyone is going to try to throw me out once the shift changes, so I better go. Besides, I don't want to overstay my welcome."

He's lucid with his jaw clenched and his shoulders held tightly in place, but his deep blue eyes are unreadable. "Avery, you need to steer clear of me for a while. They shouldn't have let you in last night."

"It figures you remember that part." Folding my arms over my chest, I look down at him. "What else do you remember, Mr. Jones?"

"Only that I said things I shouldn't have. This isn't truth serum." His hackles are rising as he points at the IV bags. Something he said has him worried. Or maybe he has no idea what he said at all.

"I won't tell your secrets."

"I don't want you to know everything."

"What? Where'd that come from? Coherent Sean is saying something forthright?" I laugh, trying to lighten the mood, but he doesn't bite.

"I mean it. There are things you shouldn't know. Ignorance protects you. Some people were made to walk alone. I'm one of them."

That's it. I've had it with his wall and I won't be pushed away again. "Bullshit. Last night you said you loved me." Sean looks away, his eyes searching desperately, avoiding my gaze. "You told me a lot of things and I told you a lot of things. I have no idea what you heard either. That's what this is about, right? That you don't know what you said? Well, the facts are that I don't know what you remember and I said things that I normally wouldn't have said to you, so we're even."

Sean's hand grips the switch and he presses the call button. The intercom clicks on, "Yes?"

"I'd like to be alone. Please escort this woman out and don't let her come back up. I need to rest." Sean says the words flatly, watching me.

My mind flashes to last night, to the pain I caused him and I wonder if this is part of that.

"Certainly, Mr. Ferro. Someone will be there in a moment." The static clicks off and I know no one is listening.

Leaning in close to his face, I bite my lips and try not to explode with anger. "That was a nasty thing to do."

"I'm a nasty person." He owns the words when they fall from his lips.

"So am I." My lips brush his on the last word and then I do it—I lean on him enough to make him scream. As his lips part, I dart my tongue inside his mouth, kissing him hard.

The door opens and I hear a nurse yell. "Don't lean on him! What's wrong with you?" She yanks me off.

Sean's eyes are crystal blue and vivid with pain, excitement, and something more. I watch him for a second as I wipe the taste of him off my mouth. "So, I guess you want me to take that job after all? It's okay. I get it, Sean. If you need me, you know who to call." It's a bluff, but I can't walk away with him thinking that I'm hurt. Using Miss Black is low, but I have no other cards to play.

The nurse is scolding me, but Sean

speaks over her. "Avery, don't." That's all he says, two words.

I turn around right before leaving the room, and smile. "What do you care?"

"I said no." He growls at me from across the room. The nurse looks from Sean to me, like we've become a tennis match.

My gaze is locked on his, utterly defiant. "Since when do I listen to what you say? Actually, you said I should stay away from you. It seems like a good plan to me. It's not like I can apply to grad school since I missed that whole graduation thing."

His face goes slack. "You missed it?"

"Graduation is next week. There's no way in Hell I passed anything. I missed the entire semester, so I won't get my credits and without them, no diploma. No grad school. No point to my entire fucking existence, so why not take that job offer? After everything is said and done, life comes down to pain and money. I have plenty of pain, so it's time to do something about the latter."

"Avery, don't test me."

"Sean, it's not a test. We're done. You said it yourself." I shove out the door and dart down the hallway, past the security guards heading to Sean's room. They have no idea that I'm the troublemaker, so I slip past them. Once I'm down the elevator and out the front door, I slow and catch my breath.

Clutching my face in my hands I bend at the waist and bite back a scream. How can he do this? Why can't he see how much we need each other? Last night should have changed all of that, but it didn't. I lean back against the brick wall and tip my head up toward the sky.

Commotion erupts inside. Just as I push off the wall, I'm slammed back into it. Sean is standing there, enraged, with his hospital robe and the IV ripped out of his arm. Blood spirals down his forearm like red ribbons.

By the time I grasp what's happening, he's in my face, hissing and holding me to the wall. "You will not work for her, not now, not ever again. Do you understand me? You're mine, Avery. I can't let you do it. I can't let you throw everything away, not for that—not for me—not for anyone." His grip slackens and I gasp, staring at him.

Nurses and doctors are trying to pull him off of me and coax him back to bed, but the man is an ox. He doesn't move if he doesn't want to. They're about to stab him with a needle and drag his ass back upstairs. No doubt the Ferro family will have to make a massive hospital contribution for his behavior.

My voice is soft, pleading. I'm done playing games. I just want to be with him. "Then, stop pushing me away."

"It's too late. You're with Scott."

"No, I'm not." They stab Sean with a needle and he roars. The people watching flinch and some visibly step back. I'm the only nut who wants to be closer. Taking his face in my hands, I turn him toward me. "I told you this last night. I'm not with him, I never was." Well, hopefully that part is true. I didn't mean to lie, but it popped out. I glaze over it, hoping to God that I haven't lied, that Trystan and I were never together. It'll hurt him so much, and I can't let him think I gave up on him and moved on, not when he was still in love with me. "Sean, I love you. I want you. The only reason I'd work for her is because you don't want me."

"I do want you. I want what you want. I want the picket fence. I want the baby. I want you. I'm just...afraid." He blinks slowly and then does it again. He's fighting the sedative, but can't. "It'll turn out the same. I can't live through that again. Avery—" Sean staggers and the burly doctors and nurses grab him when he turns to jelly. "Stay."

I watch him for a moment. A nurse tells me they have to get him back to his bed. "You can't rush out of here before you're ready."

Sean smiles lopsidedly at me. "I already did. For you, I'd do anything. Don't go to Black—don't take that job. Promise me." He reaches for me, and takes my hand.

"I won't take the job. I promise."

Chapter 8

A few days later I'm sitting in the cafeteria opposite Peter. It has been a hellish week. Bryan's funeral is in the morning. They delayed it as long as possible so Sean could attend. We're trying to figure out how to get him there since he's still too weak to do much.

Bryan's early demise caught me off guard. Sean told me about it, but it was the aftermath on the news that's made it even more hideous. "What happened?"

Peter shakes his head and stares at his coffee. "No one knows. The best they can piece together is that Bryan and Sean hated each other and it was intentional."

I make a face, "What, like Bryan committed suicide?"

"Sort of, but not. More like Bryan threw himself in the line of fire to avoid other things."

"Do you believe that?"

Peter shakes his head. "No, not if he was with Sean. The man protects his family, no matter what people say or hear. Sean wouldn't let Bryan commit suicide and there's no way Bryan killed Amanda. That's just ridiculous. He has no motive and people are speculating wildly. One theory is that Amanda was pregnant with Bryan's baby and couldn't take the guilt. She was going to tell Sean, so Bryan shot her. It's ludicrous."

I'm staring at him with my jaw hanging open. "That's the stupidest thing I've ever heard."

Peter shrugs. "People believe what they want to believe. Either way, it makes Sean look like a martyr for all these years, never saying a word about it, silently grieving his losses. The same people that were spitting on him previously, are now sending him fan mail."

"What? Seriously?" I nearly drop my paper cup of tea.

"Yeah, it's weird. There are more letters every day. You can't turn on the television without seeing how Sean was horribly wronged all these years and his little cousin got away with murder. No one seems to care that Bryan took out a mobster."

"That's horrible. Bryan was a good man," I choke up when I say his name. "I still can't believe Sean would drive him into danger."

"I don't think he would, but Sean is still medicated, so the facts are blurry. The shooting occurred and then Sean went straight from the police station to find you. He hadn't slept. It's amazing he blocked that bullet." Peter pushes back his dark hair and slumps back into his chair. His dark blue eyes bore into me, pinning me in place. "Tell me how he got it."

My gaze darts around and I feign confusion. "I don't know what you mean."

"I think you do. That gun was connected to another homicide—there was a man found in the woods. He's yet to be identified. Bryan asked you for it, didn't he?

He never told you why or he made up some bullshit story so you wouldn't tell Sean. Avery, everything has been pinned on Bryan and he's dead. If you did something, if someone tried to hurt you and you fired, it's not murder."

I laugh and smile too much. "Peter, you've been watching too much TV. Nothing like that happened."

"Really?" He raises a dark brow. "Because I happened to be up at Sean's old place and found out that someone shot out the window a while back. You wouldn't know anything about that either, right?"

I stare at him, heart pounding. For a second neither of us says a thing. "You have other people to care for and knowing what I know is like placing a bomb in your living room. Don't ask about things that you don't want to know."

Peter's gaze drops and he's silent for a while. When he looks back up he says, "I did something once, well, more than once. The guilt eats away at you if you don't let it out. Tell someone, when someone is coherent."

I smile. "Someone is trying to get out of

here every time his meds wear off. He hates this place."

"I can believe it." Peter stands. "Avery, if you need anything just ask. As far as I'm concerned, you're one of us. Sean loves you, no matter what he says. We won't let anything happen to you."

I smile. "Thanks. Where are you off to now?"

"Police station. They're canvassing the area for Masterson and he still hasn't shown up. The guy's hiding or gone. They need to shake him out before they lose him."

I startle. "They haven't caught Marty?" Every time I turn the TV on, it makes Sean angry, so I haven't been watching. I assumed they caught him.

"No." Peter tucks his hair behind his ear and looks around. "Do you have any idea why he wanted you dead? It seems so random."

"He said he loved me a while back. He pretended to be gay to be near me. I had no idea, Peter. Assuming Marty did this to begin with, the only thing I can think is that he was aiming for Sean. The whole thing is so weird. It's not like him." That topic stings horribly.

"What about your other friend? The mouthy girl with the big hair."

"Mel? Mel had nothing to do with this!" I'm defensive when I shouldn't be.

Peter puts up his hands in surrender. "All right, I'm just pointing out the obvious."

But it's not clear to me. "Spell it out for me, Peter."

"The only people you know who aren't dead are accused of murder. Mel is an anomaly."

"I only knew two people."

He gives me a look. "The sex video has sprung back to life. You know more than two people, a lot more. I know Sean can be hard, but stay here until they release him tonight. At least here I know you've got some security."

Mari walks into the cafeteria. She smiles at me and I feel guilt and shame pool in the pit of my stomach. Ever since I found out she was the woman Trystan was in love with, I feel horrible. Peter smirks. "Case in point—you know more than two people."

"Hey, Avery. How's Sean?" Mari already

knows how he's doing, but she's sweet enough to ask so I can talk about it if I want to.

"Doing better, thanks."

"I heard about Bryan." She looks at her hands. "I'm sorry for your loss. Both of you." Mari glances at Peter who stands there frozen. "I knew him a little bit, anyway. He was kind."

Peter snaps out of it. "You're welcome to attend the wake tonight, if you'd like."

She nods slowly. "I may." After a second she asks, "If Trystan won't be there. I don't want to make him more upset."

"I know I shouldn't ask, but what happened with you guys?" I can't help myself. The two of them seem perfect together, and yet they avoid each other.

She smiles softly. "We dated a long time ago. That seems like a past life. That's all. I suppose there are still some sore spots, but there's also compassion. I don't want to make it more difficult for him."

Peter offers, "If that Hummer isn't there, then Trystan isn't there. The car is usually with the man. I hope to see you later. Not many people can say anything about Bryan with conviction these days. They wonder if the man they knew was a lie."

"No, the Bryan I knew was real." Mari sounds certain. "He was hurting, but he put his friends and family first."

"How'd you know that?" I ask, blurting it out.

"The way he'd suddenly go quiet and tense up. He was either really upset or he was hurting. I assumed the latter, because Bryan didn't let things get to him. He'd laugh himself sick if he could. I've never seen a guy smile so much." She looks like she's remembering him. All three of us are silent for a moment.

Peter then gazes over at me. "If you need help with Sean, I'm here. Call me. Oh, and give me your cell number."

"Uh, I don't have one right now." Peter looks at me like I've grown a testicle on my face or something equally weird. "Sean and Trystan took my phone so I couldn't be tracked. I don't know where it is, so I don't have one at the moment."

Mari speaks up, "Here, use mine." She hands it to me.

"That's okay. I'm fine, really." I shove it back.

"I have three." Now she has balls on her face. Sighing she explains, "One is for work, one is personal, and one is a number only one person has, and since we both know that person, you can use it."

"Trystan has this number?" I ask glancing at the phone.

She nods. "I never changed it. Life is rough sometimes. I wanted to make sure he had someone if he ever needed someone. Shut up and take it, okay." Mari stands up, flustered. "I'll walk Dr., uh Ferro... Granz... Uh, I'll walk Dr. Peter out. If you want to talk, you know where to find me." Mari made sure I knew where her office was on day one.

"Thank you, Mari."

"No problem." She walks away with Peter, giving him the number before I can say anything else.

When I glance up at the TV, there's more news on the Ferro family and Marty. Marty's mother is pleading for him to come out and talk. She's afraid a sniper will take him down before he can say he's innocent.

Numbly, I stare at the show, watching her call out to her son, begging him to come forward.

Chapter 9

The next week rushes by in a blur of tears and sorrow. I still can't believe Bryan is gone, and other than the outpouring of emotion I heard from Sean the night after Bryan was killed, no one is certain what happened or why. I feel horrible for giving him that gun. Bryan told me he could change things for Sean, that the public wouldn't despise him anymore. It isn't until now that I realize he meant to do this all along.

It worked. The news has been all over the place, replaying old clips of Sean walking into the courthouse for his trial, to more current clips of him, both with that stoic expression on his lips, both taken after a loss. Instead of attacking him, they're playing Sean up to be this mysterious, sensitive man that everyone mistook. The fact that he silently took the blame for his wife's murder to protect someone else just feeds the media frenzy. It has been nonstop Ferro. The press is parked out at the mansion and at Elizabeth Ferro's lavish home.

Lucky for me, no one knows where I am, squatting in my parents old house. I managed to get the closing date from the realty company. I keep the lights off and make sure no one sees me come or go. I've replaced the broken glass on the back window. It's not technically correct, but it's enough so that if someone comes by they won't see broken glass. The pane is sloppily glued in place with Liquid Nails. If someone gets close, they can tell, but no one has been looking. The realtor doesn't come by because the house has already sold. Her commission is within reach. I just have to be out before the final walkthrough. By then, I should have a better idea of what to do next.

Sean begged me not to work for Black and I know that would be the height of stupidity, but the thought jumps around in my mind like a drunken rabbit. What if I had all the money I needed? What if I had the power to make men fall at my feet and beg? I don't like these thoughts, but they keep popping up. I wonder if I'm losing myself, if life has gotten so difficult that the true Avery has sunk beneath the waves forever.

Mari's phone buzzes. I'm lying on my back in the empty living room, staring at the ceiling. It's a text message from Peter.

Have you seen Sean?

That's a weird question. I type back.

Not since the other night. He wanted some time to do man things, alone.

What time was that?

I think for a moment and answer

Around 9pm a couple days ago. Sean's done this before. He's fine.

But as I type the words, a chill shoots up my spine, making me think something's wrong. He shouldn't have gone anywhere in his condition, but he said he had business that had to be done. I promised to hide out with Trystan, but I came here instead. I can't imagine Sean falling off the map unless he wanted to.

I'm with Mom and Aunt Lizzie pretending not to notice. They know something's up, but neither of them will say anything. Sean is in trouble. Meet me at IHOP in 20 minutes.

That explains why Sean didn't call, but I wasn't going to let myself get worked up about it. I figured he fell asleep or something. I text back a quick confirmation. Peter must know something I don't.

Pushing up, I get to my feet, careful not to stand in front of the window. Normally I wouldn't leave at this time of day. There are too many people coming and going, someone might see me. But I'm worried about Sean.

I tap his number into this old phone and wait. It rings forever. No voicemail. No nothing. Weird. I text him and don't receive a reply.

"Where are you, Sean?" The pit of my stomach sinks and for half a second I think I know where he is, but dismiss the thought. There's no way he'd be there.

Chapter 10

When I see Peter, he's in a booth with a cup of coffee in his hand. "Have you eaten?"

I shake my head. "I don't feel like it."

"Too bad, I ordered for you." He grins. "It'll be out in a second."

"So asking was meant to do what?"

His smile turns bashful and he sighs. "You're hard to read, so I tossed out a direct question, which you answered, which is what I figured you'd say. If Sean hasn't seen you in a couple of days, I seriously doubt you ate, especially with everything that's been going on. Here it is now." Peter leans back as several waitresses trail after each other, single file, placing dish after dish on the table.

"You ordered everything on the menu?" I salivate as I stare at a stack of pancakes. The scent of bacon hits me and my stomach grumbles.

"I didn't know what you liked." Peter says it seriously, which makes me laugh.

"There's everything, except coffee."

"Yeah, I only share coffee with Sidney." He blushes and dips his head, grabbing a plate of eggs.

"Did you just make a dirty joke?" I can't help it, I smile and it feels good. The muscles feel stiff and unused.

"Perhaps. Eat and let's talk about Sean." He points a fork at me and we start to backtrack through his days, trying to figure out what he was doing or where he went.

I finally blurt it out, because he's got to be thinking it, too. "What if Sean went after Marty?"

Peter glances up. "Sean wouldn't, not in his condition and not without me."

"He tried to take on Campone alone."

"He had Bryan." Peter's voice becomes stiff. He drops his fork and looks at me.

"What do you think is happening?"

"I think Marty has him holed up somewhere. Maybe Sean went after Marty. Maybe Sean found him. We both know Sean isn't at the top of his game right now. It gave Marty the upper hand. So if Sean's plan didn't work out, Marty could be holding him somewhere—waiting for me. He's been trying to get at me all this time. It's the perfect bait. He knows I won't leave Sean. He even told me to work for..." I trail off before I say Miss Black's name. Something pings in the back of my brain, but I can't put the pieces together.

Peter glazes over it, and leans back in the booth before he shakes his head. "Masterson wouldn't take the risk."

"You're wrong there. He totally would." My voice has grown soft and I have that spaced out look people get when they're trying to find the square root of 3.

A moment of silence passes and a forkful of pancakes is dangling halfway between the plate and my mouth. Is there a connection somewhere? Did I miss it? Does Marty know Black? He couldn't.

"Care to share?"

"Huh?" I drop my fork and it clatters on the plate, knocking the bits of breakfast loose. They fall on the table.

Peter smiles and leans forward. "You're on to something and not telling me. Please tell me you're not as stubborn as Sean." I laugh without meaning to. "Fuck."

"Yeah, I'm more stubborn than Sean. And something is bouncing around in my head, but it's just a feeling. I can't make a connection."

Peter extends his hand, gesturing to me to share. "Lay it on me. Maybe we can make the connection together."

"Marty and my former employer, what if they wanted to get back at me?"

Peter shifts in his seat and leans in close. With a low voice he asks, "The madam? Why would she want to get back at you through Sean?"

"I don't know. She could have gone straight for me. There were enough times that she could have hurt me if she wanted to." I've latched onto the right combination. I know it. I just can't see how the whole mess fits together. "You're right, Peter. Something's wrong." Flicking my eyes up to his, I ask, "What's your mom saying?"

"Nothing. She's acting like everything is fine, but it's not because Aunt Lizzie is there. Mom never calls her, not unless there's some serious stuff going down."

"So, they know something."

"I assume they have an idea, yes. The thing is, they won't show their cards until their hand is played."

"So, we'll have to force them to tell us."

Peter has an incredulous look on his face. "You can't force Mother to do a damned thing. Where do you think Sean gets it? The plotting and scheming, the secrecy, it's all part of our mother's personality. When things get rough, she puts up a barricade and no one will get through." Peter downs the rest of his orange juice and drops money on the table. "Come on."

I jump up and follow him outside. When he pushes through the door a gust of wind catches it and nearly smacks me in the face. "Peter!"

"Sorry, I didn't mean to do that." He holds the door for me and then walks next to me as we cross the parking lot to his car. "It's just that Sean wouldn't abandon any of us, and we both know something is off, so where would Masterson take him?"

I think for a moment, and then say the only place I can think of, "Captree, but the boat basin is going to be busy now. Marty liked to hang out down there in the winter when it was quiet."

"Let's try it anyway. It's our only lead." Peter opens a door for me and I slip into his car. It's a little black coupe with an identity crisis—I can't tell if it's an old dude car or a sports car. It's conflicted, like Peter. He can't deny he's a Ferro, but he doesn't want to be a part of that family. I can tell. He rarely mentions Sidney and the two of them try to keep their distance, but something happens to the family and he's there. Peter can't leave them—and neither can I.

Chapter 11

It's late by the time we make it to the docks. We've walked around for a while and asked people if anyone saw Sean down here, or Marty. That tactic isn't working and it's getting dark. "Peter, he's not here. Marty wouldn't choose a public place like this. I just couldn't think of any other place he'd hide out."

At the same time, we both glance up, and across the water to Oak Island and the rows of empty houses. "I bet he's over there."

"So, how do we find him?" Peter asks, leaning back against his car. The wind blows and lifts his dark hair off his face, revealing the same intense gaze Sean wears so often. "I don't know any Girl Scouts selling cookies right now."

I laugh at him. "Marty isn't going to open the door for cookies. That's something a five-year-old would do."

"Well, I'd get caught pretty quickly then, assuming I ever go for the life of crime. I can't live without cookies." Peter sounds completely serious.

Smiling, I stare at the water, watching the setting sun glint off the surface. We're quiet for a few moments before I ask, "Wait, what did you say?"

"I can't live without cookies." Peter offers that crooked grin of his and pushes off his car.

"It has been close to two weeks since the shooting. He'll have to have bought food somewhere."

Peter shakes his head. "If the guy is holding out in one of those houses, he could have picked one that was stocked. And if the guy is an evil mastermind, he's not going to come out for food. He would have had it stashed before he went to the concert and revealed himself."

We talk more, and finally get in the car again, driving up and down the highway. We talk, but it leads to nothing and it's way past twilight. Peter slams his palms on the steering wheel and swears. There's that Ferro temper. It's hard to picture Peter being the guy he used to be, polar opposite of what he is now. It makes me wonder if Sean has a chance to pull his life together too.

I finally blurt out, "I can call him."

"Who? Marty Masterson?"

"Are you stuck in teacher mode or something? Marty Masterson." I mimic him and smile. Teasing Peter is fun. "The guy was my friend. We don't have to use his last name."

"There's no way he has his phone on him." Peter shakes his head as he drives. The water passes swiftly beneath us as we pass over the bridge.

"But I bet he has his phone forwarding to somewhere. If I call him from my phone, he'll answer. I can find out if he has Sean." I glance over at Peter. "What other choices do we have?"

"Where's your phone?"

"Trystan hid it."

Peter glances at me. "I don't want Scott involved in this and you know if we call him, there's no way to get rid of him."

"I know." I feel horrible about it, but I need the phone. "The other option is to take the job with Black and see what shakes out. If this is leverage, they have me either way."

"You really think they're in this together?"

"I don't know."

"I don't see it, but you've spent more time around them than me. I say we try to call Marty first."

"Let's do it."

Chapter 12

Tracking down Trystan isn't hard. He's with Jon at the club. When we get there, Trystan lets us in and waits. He acts like it's totally normal for Peter to be here, driving me around. It's possible that he's mad at me, but I can't tell. Trystan is hard to read when he's upset. He's so used to putting on a public mask that it hardly ever comes off. Either way, he's got to be wondering why Peter is with me.

Peter is tense, though he tries to hide it, and Trystan is lounging in a chair like we're on a cruise. Peter didn't tell Trystan much, but he already figured it out. Some of the tabloids claim he's not that bright, but

Trystan hides his intelligence. It's a card he'll play last, when everything else has failed. In the meantime, very few people know him at all.

"So what's the plan? Are you seriously going to let her walk into wherever they're keeping Sean? If Black's in on it—"

I stop and stare at him, trying to remember if I ever said her name. I can't remember mentioning it, so how does he know her name? "Trystan!" I scold; I'm suddenly concerned Black's reach is further than I dreamed. "Tell me you didn't!"

"I don't need hookers, Call Girl."

Rolling my eyes, I place my hands on my hips and give him the evil eye. "I know you don't need them, but did you use her services? For anything?"

He looks away and my stomach drops into my shoes. Mouth gaping, Peter intercedes. "Trystan lives here, and if he called for a high-dollar call girl, there is no one else. He would have contacted Black. The reason isn't important right now. When's the last time you used her services?" Peter tries to gloss over it, but I can't stand it.

Trystan tries to get up and walk away without answering, but I catch him by the wrist. "Why didn't you tell me?"

"Does it matter?" His gaze is hiding something, humiliation perhaps? His hair falls forward and Trystan leaves it covering his dark eyes.

"Yes, it matters. You're another connection back to that awful woman. Did she tell you to buddy up to me? Tell me, Trystan, does she have your balls in a glass jar along with the balls of every other man on Long Island?" I'm in his face, hissing the words. Trystan doesn't walk away or deny it. Instead he just stands there watching me, waiting for me to give up on him. It's infuriating. "Stop it!" My hand swings and the slap connects with his cheek. I tremble for a second and watch him. He doesn't fight back, which kills me.

He smiles. "Are you happy now?"

"Trystan, I—"

"Avery, he's not the one you're mad at. Let it go." Peter is standing next to me, ready to pull me away.

"But he—"

"Leave it alone. You're missing pieces of

this story—anyone can see that. Trystan isn't using you, and if he were a repeat customer of a call girl service the press would have picked up on it by now. Let it go. We need to find Sean and we can't do that with you two fighting, so stop."

Trystan is smirking. He leans to the side to catch my eye. "I know Pete said to leave it alone, but this really makes me wonder how you could be such a hypocrite. You condemn me so quickly even though you're on the taking end of this deal. Liars are we, twisting the truth until it suits us best? Life's a bitch, isn't it?"

Peter gives Trystan a look that promises a punch in the face if he doesn't stop. Even so, I can't leave it alone.

"I'm not a liar or a hypocrite. That's not why I'm upset. It's because you know Miss Black. Admit it. You've met her. There's no way you haven't. Then I pour my heart out to you, assuming you have no connection to her and the entire time you already knew her and didn't correct me. Did you know that she knows Sean, too? Did you know that every time I turn around, I expect to see her there, waiting to pull me back? Did you know I don't have a choice? She won't let me leave, Trystan! I'm caught in the middle of her fucking vortex and I can't get out. But you already know all that don't you?" Tears are in my eyes and I look away, feeling betrayed. I try to hide it. I can't fall apart now, no matter what he's done.

Trystan runs his hands through his hair, revealing his toned midriff, before blurting out, "I use her services once a year. It's to forget about *her*. How am I supposed to confess something like that, when it's so damning? Now Pete knows, which means it's not a secret anymore. It'll spread and the next time I see Mari, she'll hate me even more." He's smiling like it's funny, but his words are so somber that I feel my gut twisting inside of me.

Peter watches the two of us closely, but he doesn't comment. It probably looks like we're in a relationship, but we're not. I need friends, I can't survive without them, and Trystan said he'd always be there for me. Marty uttered the same words and now look what's happened. Who can I trust?

Trystan slumps down on a beat up couch, while Peter starts to pace the room.

Peter stops and glances over at me. Concern etches his face, increasing the depth of the fine worry lines. He thinks he's going to lose his brother. I can see that fear; I know what he's thinking because the same thoughts have been filling my mind since Peter surfaced. Peter doesn't show up without a reason and he tends to bolt as soon as possible. I can't blame him, not with the Ferro family. It's no mystery why Sidney isn't here—Peter's afraid—and so am I.

All three of us are silent for a moment. That's when Mel and Jon come out of the office. Jon is somber, but his expression changes when he sees us. "What the fuck is this?" Jon's been so mad since Bryan died. His anger is always just below the surface, ready to erupt.

Trystan leans back into the couch without answering and Peter looks down at his saddle shoes, so Mel and Jon both turn their attention to me.

Mel is wearing sweats and gold hoop earrings. Her hair has expanded to twice its normal size. The look is very odd for a girl who is always perfectly dressed. She looks like a hot hobo. "Staring at the floor means they're up to no good. A big chunk of stupid fell and hit them on the head, Jonny boy. There's no way you can keep me from finding out what's going on so you might as well spill."

Jon is staring at me with an unreadable expression. I can't tell if he's mad or something worse. Finally, he sighs and runs his hands through his hair and down his neck. He glances at Peter. "It's Sean, right?" Peter's gaze flicks up, surprised. Jon rolls his eyes. "Pete, I notice things. Mom and Aunt Lizzie have been together way too much. Something's up, and it's major. Plus, Sean is ominously absent. It's a very strange combo, especially since Sean likes to put his nose in everything. Bossing people around is his specialty and for some reason, he's not here protecting Avery the way he should be, and since Bryan's dead, well, we know he's not there either."

I can't help it. I snap at him, "It wasn't Sean's fault."

Jon looks down and I can see the wall go up as his eyes turn to steel. "Just answer my fucking question—what's wrong?"

Peter sighs and looks over at me. I nod

and clutch my middle tighter as Peter tells them our suspicion, and then the phone call. Jon retains his stern look and pointed focus. "Leave him."

Peter, Trystan, Mel, and I all speak in unison. "What?"

Jon shrugs, like it's not a big deal. "Sean got himself into this, he can get himself out."

"Jon," Peter speaks with that deep voice that almost sounds like a scold.

"Don't talk to me like that Pete. Sean did this. It's his mistake and there's not a fucking chance in Hell that any of you should go pay for it. Masterson is a lunatic. He'll kill both of you, Avery. If he's responsible for all those murders—"

I cut him off, "Yeah, *if.* Jon, he can't be, Marty's not like that. He doesn't fight and he hardly ever loses his temper. It's weird."

"How can you say that? You saw the gun in his hand!" Jon's temper is rising and it feels like I'm poking a pissed off bear while covered in honey. It's the dumbass thing to do, but something's wrong and we have to find Sean.

"I saw it, I know, but I can't believe it."

Jon starts to laugh at me, like I'm too naïve to breathe. Getting in his face, I sternly add, "I can't believe it just like I don't believe Sean killed Amanda. The same way I don't believe for a second that Bryan was a scheming, malicious man. There's something you don't know, something that will make you hate me, but I have to tell you —you need to know."

Peter's eyes are wide. He holds up his hands and shakes his head. "Avery, don't!"

"I have to. It's my fault." Glancing back at his brother, I confess, "Jon, I gave Bryan the gun. If you're going to be pissed at someone for everything that happened, I did it, not Sean. Be mad at me." Regret nearly tears my chest in half. I can't stand the way they're all looking at me. I didn't know that Bryan would do what he did. Being the man he was, Bryan would have done it anyway, gun or not. He loved Hallie too much to leave her to Victor.

Jon's eyes glow like twin flames, bright blue and deadly. "You gave it to him? You mean, all the shit that's been following Sean around was laid on my cousin because you gave him the fucking gun!" Jon is screaming, his face red with rage.

Peter jumps between us because Jon is way too close. Trystan is up and tugging Jon back, but this needs to happen. Jon wants to blame someone for his best friend's death and he needs to blame me. Gently, I put my hand on Peter's shoulder and step around him.

"Avery." There's a warning tone in Pete's voice.

Trystan gives a gentle shake of his head, indicating that I shouldn't say anything else, but I have to. I never told any of them and guilt is tearing me apart. Besides, directing his anger at Sean is wrong when I'm the one to blame.

My voice is soft. I won't fight with him. "I can't let you think that Sean caused this, because he didn't. If Bryan didn't have the gun, none of the stuff with Victor would have happened. I spun things into motion. Jon, I'm sorry. Please believe me when I say that Sean didn't know. He truly didn't."

Jon watches me closely, trying to decide if I'm lying. Hallie calls out behind him, she must have been in the office too. "Jon, how do you want this to end?" He turns on his heel and looks back at her. Hallie looks weary but fierce, standing there in jeans and a ratty t-shirt, her thick hair pulled back into a ponytail. "You lost Bryan, but you don't have to lose Sean too."

"You really think Masterson has him? If he does, will he kill Sean? Is this even about Sean?" Jon asks, glaring at me with his icy eyes flicking up to meet mine. The room is eerily quiet. They want to know what would turn a lovable guy into a homicidal maniac, but the truth is as unfathomable to me as it is to them.

"I don't know. Marty's lied to me before —like huge-ass lies—and I forgave him. Maybe he thinks I'll forgive this. I don't know, no one knows what happened that night. They think Marty took the shot, because he had a gun—and then he ran. Running doesn't mean he did it." I glance at Mel, who's been way too quiet. Normally, she would have interrupted and given her opinion by now. "What do you think?"

"I think Marty's been playing you, Avery. And I seriously doubt that he has Sean. Think about it, even injured, I can't see Sean Ferro getting kidnapped by Marty. It's too much of a stretch. A fucking pacifist caught shooting a Ferro at a megastar concert?" She shakes her head, making her huge-ass earrings swing. "Fishy, sister, and not the kind of fishy funk that goes away with some Monistat."

We all make a face, but Peter's the one who talks. "Lovely comparison."

She smirks. "It ain't white boy poetry, but I could write books—novels about the shit I seen—so don't judge me. I talk the way I talk because this is the real me. I never forgot where I resided prior to my education, and it's ingrained so deeply in my bones that they're etched with that past life. What you are witnessing now is a manifestation of the past and the present colliding." The boys' expressions are incredulous, as if they can't believe Mel knew words with more than two syllables. She folds her arms over her chest, snaps gum I didn't realize she was chewing and throws her hip out. "Like I was saying, you can't change who you are. We either pegged that son of a bitch wrong, or someone's playin' us. I, for one, don't give a shit about Sean, but I know Avery does, so I'm here.

Whatever you need, we'll find him." She smiles softly at me and places her hand on my shoulder.

No one says anything for a moment. Mel's message is clear—Marty Masterson could be putting on an act that never ends. I know Mel could play corporate colored woman if she wanted to and deal with the daily drivel that goes with it. She has the intelligence; she simply chooses not to show it. So, here she is with us, in a strip club on Long Island, instead of in a power suit, kicking corporate ass in the city.

"So, we pretend Marty is innocent until we know he's not?" I ask Mel, to make sure I caught her meaning.

"Rule number one: Don't make enemies." She ticks off a finger then holds up another, "Rule number two: When you do, take them down first. And Avery, it's a matter of when, not if, because it's easy for people to hate. Even if there's no reason, some fuckers are hell-bent on finding one. Marty ain't what he seems, and never was. He played us once, so why not twice? We should have cut him off already. I didn't because you didn't. I don't give people second chances. Forgiving only gets you hurt—or dead." The way she says it is so calloused, so unfeeling. We're talking about someone who shared drinks and slept over. Marty kept me safe when no one else was around. I slept in his arms and he chased away my demons.

Shaking my head, I wrap my arms around my middle and say to the floor, "It's so hard to believe."

Jon's calmed down enough to speak, but he doesn't look at me. "There's a manhunt for Masterson and he's not been caught yet. That says the fucker is smarter than anyone thought. The problem we have right now is Sean. Stay focused."

Trystan nods. "Something big is going on. I'm wondering if I'm part of it, and how far this whole thing has spread. I get why Sean asked me to watch you the other night. At the time it seemed like an ass move, but he went to help Hallie and Bryan. Something went wrong. Bryan took the shot and cleared him. Now Sean is missing. Any chance all this shit is connected? I feel like we're missing something."

My ringtone fills the air before anyone

can answer. It's coming from Trystan's pocket. He pulls it out and the expression on his face scares me. "I think we're about to find out. It's Sean."

As he speaks the phone flies through the air in a high arc. I catch it and stare at Sean's picture on the screen. Nerves twist me up so quickly that my palms are already sweaty and my stomach twists like I'm in a freefall. The phone rings again. All eyes are on me waiting.

Chapter 13

I try to hide the fear that's choking me. There's no way he's fine—I know it before I answer. This call is an omen, and there's no escaping what's to come. Trembling, I swipe the screen and then press the phone to my ear. "Where have you been? Sean, I've worried myself sick." I can't hide the quiver in my voice. I wait for him to reply and only hope that someone hasn't hurt him. Whoever took down Sean must be more powerful, more skillful at deception and a better fighter. I can't imagine who it could be. Black is the only person who comes to mind. I half expect him to say that she's behind everything, so when the voice hits my ear, I'm paralyzed.

Marty's voice is strong and clear. "Awh, how sweet. You do care, and here I thought it would never happen. Silly me."

The room is quiet, all eyes on me. Fear races through my veins, and rushes into my heart. "Why do you have Sean's phone? Marty, I swear to God, if you hurt him—"

"What, you'll girly-punch me?" He laughs lightly, like we're still friends before continuing. "Avery, babe, I'm up for any kink you want to play out, but I need to finish what we started. The thing is I've decided to live a little, you know. If I'm going to chance getting caught, I should have the woman I want in the mix. So, sweet face, grab some food for us, and a few bandages for your boyfriend here. He wasn't being nice, so I may have opened some of his stitches—but only a little. The thing is, he's staining the carpet. Some people are so inconsiderate. Anyway, bring one bag of eats and your pretty little ass—and only your pretty little ass—to the old parking area for the Oak Beach Inn. You have an hour. Don't disappoint me." The line goes dead and I stare at the phone in my hand.

Everyone is waiting for me to repeat what I heard. Numbness consumes me as betrayal cracks my heart. He did it. He took the shots—it has been him all along and I've been defending him.

"Well?" Mel impatiently prods.

"Marty has Sean."

NEW RELEASES

To ensure you don't miss H.M. Ward's next book, text AWESOMEBOOKS (one word) to 22828 and you will get an email reminder on release day.

**

Want to talk to other fans?
Go to Facebook and join the discussion!

COMING SOON

BROKEN PROMISES
A Trystan Scott Novel

MORE FERRO FAMILY BOOKS

NICK FERRO
~THE WEDDING CONTRACT~
*****

BRYAN FERRO
~THE PROPOSITION~
*****

SEAN FERRO
~THE ARRANGEMENT~
******

PETER FERRO GRANZ
~DAMAGED~
******

JONATHAN FERRO
~STRIPPED~
******

TRYSTAN SCOTT
~COLLIDE~
*****

MORE ROMANCE BOOKS BY H.M. WARD

DAMAGED

DAMAGED 2

STRIPPED

SCANDALOUS

SCANDALOUS 2

SECRETS

THE SECRET LIFE OF TRYSTAN SCOTT

And more.

To see a full book list, please visit:
www.SexyAwesomeBooks.com/books.htm

CAN'T WAIT FOR H.M. WARD'S NEXT STEAMY BOOK?

⭐⭐⭐⭐⭐

Let her know by leaving stars and telling her
what you liked about
THE ARRANGEMENT 16
in a review!